Puffin

TALES FROM ALL
SCHO

There's never a dull moment at Allotment Lane
School, especially in Miss Mee's class. Ian picks up
various oddments on the way to school and finds they
all come in useful. Jean can't have a birthday party at
home, so Miss Mee arranges one for her at school, and
Nasreen and Asif are busy making giant, man-eating
spiders when something very odd happens at
Hallowe'en.

Twelve lively, colourful stories to read aloud or to
read alone. Life is fun, full and busy at Allotment Lane
School.

Margaret Joy was born on Tyneside. After living for
some years on Teesside, where she taught in a VI-form
college and later became a teacher of five year olds, she
moved to North Wales, where her husband is headmaster of a school for deaf children. They have four
children. Margaret Joy has contributed a number of
stories to BBC TV *Play School* and BBC Radio's
Listen with Mother.

Other books by Margaret Joy

ALLOTMENT LANE SCHOOL AGAIN
HAIRY AND SLUG
SEE YOU AT THE MATCH

Margaret Joy

Tales from
Allotment Lane School

Illustrated by Rowena Allen

PUFFIN BOOKS
in association with
Faber and Faber

Puffin Books, Penguin Books Ltd, Harmondsworth, Middlesex, England
Viking Penguin Inc., 40 West 23rd Street, New York, New York 10010, U.S.A.
Penguin Books Australia Ltd, Ringwood, Victoria, Australia
Penguin Books Canada Ltd, 2801 John Street, Markham, Ontario, Canada L3R 1B4
Penguin Books (N.Z.) Ltd, 182–190 Wairau Road, Auckland 10, New Zealand

First published by Faber and Faber Limited 1983
Published in Puffin Books 1985
Reprinted 1986, 1987

Made and printed in Great Britain by
Richard Clay Ltd, Bungay, Suffolk

for my family

Contents

I

Ian's Useful Collection

Miss Mee taught the youngest children at Allotment Lane School. There were about twenty children in her class and one of them was a boy called Ian. Now Ian was most particular about his trousers and *always* had pockets in them. Whenever he had new trousers he always said, 'I don't mind if they're short trousers to my knees or long trousers to my ankles. I don't mind if they're red or green or brown. But they *must* have pockets.'

The boy's name was Ian. And can you guess why Ian had to have pockets? It was to keep things in, of course. But he didn't just keep a clean hanky in them—oh, no!

Ian was a collector, just like the rest of his family. His father collected screws and nails. If he saw any curly screws or sharp nails lying about, he would pick them up and look at them and say, 'They might just come in useful.' Then he would keep them in his tool box.

Ian's mother was a collector too. She collected clean paper bags. Whenever she brought shopping home, she would take the things out of their paper bags and say, 'What lovely clean paper bags. They might just come in useful.' Then she would smooth them out and put them on top of all the other clean paper bags in the kitchen drawer.

Ian's big sister was another collector. She collected pictures of pop stars and stuck them all over the walls of her bedroom. Whenever she saw a picture or poster in a magazine, she would say, 'Cor, that's a great picture. That'll just do for my collection.' Then she would run upstairs and try to find a space for it on her bedroom wall.

Ian didn't collect screws or nails, *or*

paperbags, *or* pictures of pop stars. He collected anything at all that was interesting and fitted into his trouser pockets. When he was very, very little he once collected a pocketful of snow! You can guess what happened to that, can't you?

One morning Ian set out for school. He had clean trousers on, so his pockets were quite empty. He walked along, as he usually did, with his head bent so that he could look for interesting things on the ground as he walked along.

The first thing he spotted was a strong, thick rubber band. He knew who dropped rubber bands—the post woman! She often walked along the road with a bundle of letters, and Ian had seen her slip the rubber band off the bundle and drop it on the path. He picked it up and put it in his pocket.

Next he saw a very flat, round pebble. It was like the pebbles Ian had seen on the beach at the seaside. It was lovely to hold, cool and smooth, and Ian put it in his other pocket.

He walked a little further, still looking. Then he noticed a silver safety pin. It was shining in the sunshine and wasn't at all dirty or rusty, so Ian picked it up and put it in the pocket with the rubber band.

The next thing his sharp eyes noticed was a matchbox. It was quite clean and new. Ian opened it and sniffed. It smelt just like matches: a funny smell that made his nose wrinkle. He was very pleased with the empty matchbox, and he put it into the pocket with the rubber band and the safety pin.

He nearly missed seeing a long piece of green string near the hedge. He picked it up and rolled it round his fingers and put it in the pocket with the smooth, cool pebble. Now he was nearly at the school gate. He began to jog along, kicking a tiny broken piece of red brick in front of him. Then he thought, 'I suppose that might come in useful too.' So he picked it up and put it in the pocket with the rubber band and the safety pin and the matchbox. Now he had collected six things on the way to school and he was very pleased with himself. He ran into the playground feeling very cheerful.

Now you'll hardly believe it, but every single thing in Ian's pockets came in useful that day in school. It happened like this.

When Ian went into the classroom, the first person he saw was Miss Mee, watering the daffodils in their bowls. 'They're getting rather tall, poor things,' she said. 'We'll have to tie them to a stick so they don't bend right over.' She fetched a very old paintbrush that wasn't used any more.

'You can tie them with my string,' said Ian.

'Just the thing,' said Miss Mee, and she tied the daffodils to the stick with Ian's piece of green string.

After that Laura's skirt strap came loose. She came to show Miss Mee. 'My Mum'll kill me!' said Laura.

'Of course she won't!' said Miss Mee. 'We'll mend it somehow.' She looked round, wondering how to mend it.

'You can pin it together with my safety pin,' said Ian.

'Just the thing,' said Miss Mee, and she pinned Laura's skirt strap to the skirt with Ian's shiny, silver safety pin.

Not long before playtime Mary felt a bit sick. She said she felt too hot and had a headache. Miss Mee told her to sit down and rest her head on the table. 'You can put my nice smooth pebble next to your head, if you like,' offered Ian.

'Just the thing,' said Miss Mee, and Mary thought that was a good idea too. She held the cool flat pebble next to her hot forehead. It cheered her up a lot.

During playtime Michael's tooth came out. He brought it in to show Miss Mee.

She said he should take it home to put under his pillow. 'I might lose it,' said Michael.

'You can put it in my matchbox, if you like,' said Ian.

'Just the thing,' said Miss Mee, and Michael put his little white baby tooth into Ian's clean matchbox.

Afterwards they went into the play-ground. Miss Mee showed them how to play hopscotch on the big flagstones. 'First you have to write numbers on the stones,' she said. 'Bother! I've not brought any chalk outside with me. Could you go inside and get me a piece, Ian?'

'You can use my bit of red brick, if you like,' said Ian showing Miss Mee his little piece of red stone.

'Just the thing,' said Miss Mee and she scratched the numbers in red on the grey flagstones.

I wonder if you know what Ian had left in his pocket now?

Everyone came indoors after that. Today it was Ian's turn for painting. He loved painting and he took ages over it. When it was finished and dry, Miss Mee held it up for everyone to see, and Ian showed them the Batmobile, and Batman and Robin driving away from Catwoman. Everyone thought it was a great picture. Miss Mee rolled it up very carefully and gave it to Ian to carry home. Ian took the strong, thick rubber band out of his picket and Miss Mee helped him to put it round his lovely picture.

'Just the thing!' said Ian and Miss Mee together, and they both laughed.

2
Staying In

One winter's morning there was a thick frost on the grass. Everything outside was glittering silver in the winter sunshine, but it was still cold.

Miss Mee's children were working hard in their warm classroom. Some were doing adding up sums; others were measuring the tables. Some children were writing or drawing; others were doing puzzles or playing Number Snap. Everybody was busy.

Laura looked at the clock. The little hand was at ten, and the big hand was nearly at six. She knew that meant it was nearly half past ten—and that meant playtime. Laura looked out at the silver frost on the grass, and shivered. It was so warm and cosy in the classroom.

'I've got a headache,' she said to Miss Mee, holding her forehead. 'I'd better stay in until it's better.'

Laura's friend was Mary, and Mary heard her tell Miss Mee about her headache. She looked at the cold silver frost on the grass outside, then she looked at Laura. 'I've got a headache too,' she said, making a dreadful face to show how it was hurting her. Sue looked at her two friends. She wanted to stay in and carry on with her colouring.

'Oh, Miss Mee,' she gasped, suddenly holding her tummy. 'I've got a tummy ache. I think I'd better stay in too.'

Asif held up his knee for Miss Mee to see the red scab. 'I fell over last week—I don't think I'd better go out either.'

Paul said, 'The weather forecast on the radio said there was going to be rain later. I'd better stay in, in case it rains, because I've not brought my wellies.'

Jean growled a cough, a horribly growly cough, and said, 'My Mum said I

had to stay in with my throat when it was cold.'

Ian thought it looked cold outside too. He said, 'Miss Mee, can I stay in and help to tidy up, can I, Miss Mee?'

Nearly everybody wanted to tell Miss Mee why they needed to stay in. Then the bell went for playtime. It was suddenly quite quiet in the classroom. Only six people were waiting to go outside and play.

Miss Mee opened the drawer in her desk and said, 'Oh, look, here's that box of jelly babies I've been saving!' Everybody smiled and looked at each other and waited to see what Miss Mee was going to do with the jelly babies. She opened the box and rustled the paper.

'I don't think I'd better give one to you, Laura,' she said, looking at Laura with a very grave face. 'It might make your headache worse, and yours too, Mary, and they might make tummy aches and sore throats worse too! I'll just give a jelly baby to all the people getting ready to go out to play—they'll enjoy eating them outside in the sunshine.'

She offered the box to Gary and he chose a black jelly baby; Barbara and Rosemary both chose red ones; little Larry chose a green one to match his gloves; Nasreen took an orange one; Michael chose yellow because he liked the taste of lemon.

'Six sweets for six people going outside,' said Miss Mee. She peeped inside the box. 'Ooh, there are just a few more left...'

Suddenly, she found Mary and Laura and Sue next to her. 'Our aches are gone,' they said, nodding at each other, and they each chose a sweet and skipped out to play.

Asif limped over to Miss Mee and showed her the scab on his knee. 'I think it's nearly better now,' he said, and chose a black jelly baby and went out.

Paul looked up at the sky and said, 'It

doesn't look so much like rain now; perhaps I will chance it and go out after all.' He chose a red jelly baby and went out.

Jean gave another terrible growly cough and said, 'I think a jelly baby would help my bad throat, Miss Mee.' So Miss Mee offered her a sweet too.

All the others decided they'd like to go out in the fresh air now, and they each took a jelly baby as they went. Then only Ian was left. 'I'd still like to stay in and tidy up, Miss Mee, can I? Can I?'

'Of course you can, Ian,' said Miss Mee. 'Thank you very much.—And when you've finished, you'd better tidy up this last jelly baby. Do you think you can?' Do you think he did?

3
Mary's Busy Morning

Miss Mee put down her red pen and her black pen. She had just finished marking the register. Suddenly the door opened and in burst Mary.

'I'm sorry I'm late. The alarm clock didn't go off and the baby put her cereal plate on her head and when Mum had wiped that up she could only find me a blue sock and a red sock and then the bacon burnt and then I was running to school and a dog chased me and I fell in the mud, so I had to go home and Mum cleaned me up, so I'm late!'

Mary stood next to Miss Mee, looking so worried, and puffing and panting so much like a bicycle pump that everyone laughed. Miss Mee put her arm round poor Mary. 'Never mind,' she said. 'You're not usually late, are you?' Mary shook her head and looked a bit more cheerful. 'But I thought you were going to be away from school today, so I've marked the register. You'd better go along to Mrs Hubb—Gary can go with you—and ask for her little bottle of white stuff that hides mistakes in the register. Say: "Please, Mrs Hubb, can Miss Mee borrow the bottle of correcting fluid?" Can you remember that?'

Gary and Mary nodded and went out. They walked along to Mrs Hubb's tiny room. It was always very busy in there. She was sitting in front of her typewriter with piles of dinner money all round her and a stack of envelopes she was sticking stamps on.

Mrs Hubb looked over the top of her glasses at Mary and Gary. 'Hello, Pinky and Perky,' she said. 'What can I do for you?'

Mary took a deep breath and said, 'Please Mrs Hubb can Miss Mee borrow ... er ... um ...' She stopped.

'The bottle of correcting fluid,' said Gary, who had a very good memory.

'Yes, of course she can,' said Mrs Hubb. 'But just before you take it back to her, could you just pop into the kitchen for me and give a message to Mrs Eccles? Say: "Mrs Hubb says the cabbages will be delivered on Thursday."'

Mary and Gary had never been inside the school kitchen before, but they shyly knocked at the door and went in. All round were huge shining silver cookers. A cloud of steam was rolling up in one corner and there was a lovely warm smell of cooking. Mrs Eccles, the cook, came towards them in her white overall and white hat.

'Hello there, Topsy and Tim,' she said. 'What can I do for you?'

'Mrs Hubb said the cabbages ... er...' began Mary.

'Will be delivered on Thursday,' said Gary.

'Oh good,' said Mrs Eccles. 'Well now, I wonder if you two could just go outside to Mr Loftus and tell him that the kitchen bins need emptying. Please could he come as soon as possible.'

Gary and Mary went out into the playground, where Mr Loftus was mending a fence. 'Hello, Tom and Jerry,' he said. 'Want me, do you?'

'Yes,' nodded Mary. 'Mrs Eccles says please can you come as soon as possible.'

'Oh, what's the problem?' asked Mr Loftus.

'Er ... um ...' said Mary.

'It's the kitchen bins,' said Gary. 'They need emptying.'

'Righto!' said Mr Loftus. 'I'll see to it. Now could you take this pullover along to Mrs Owthwaite's class? It belongs to one of her Big Boys. It's been out on the grass all night—it's sopping wet.' He handed Mary a very damp grey pullover.

Gary and Mary went indoors and along to Mrs Owthwaite's classroom.

They walked in. All the Big Boys and Girls were working, but they looked up when Gary and Mary walked across to Mrs Owthwaite's table. 'Hello, Tweedledum and Tweedledee!' said Mrs Owthwaite. What's this you've got?'

'It's a pullover from ... from...' began Mary.

'From Mr Loftus,' said Gary. 'It's been out on the grass all night.'

'I'll soon find out who that belongs to,' said Mrs Owthwaite. 'Thank you very much for bringing it along. Are you just going back to Miss Mee's class? Could you tell her she's left her car lights on? I can see them in the car park, still shining.'

Gary and Mary went back along the corridor to their own classroom. Mary gave Miss Mee the little bottle of correcting fluid. 'Hello, Gary and Mary,' said Miss Mee. 'You've been ages. Where *have* you been?'

Gary took a deep breath and said, 'We

went to Mrs Hubb and asked for cabbages, then we went to Mrs Eccles with a damp pullover, then we asked Mr Loftus for a bottle of correcting fluid, then we asked Mrs Owthwaite to empty the kitchen bins, then we came back here!'

Miss Mee looked at him. 'Are you *sure* that's right, Gary?' she asked.

'Nearly,' said Gary. He thought for a moment. 'There was something else,' he said. 'Mrs Owthwaite said she could see ... er ... um'. He stopped.

'Your car in the car park with its lights on,' said Mary.

'*Oh*,' said Miss Mee. 'Thank you for telling me. What a good thing you've both got such good memories!'

4
Hunt the Caterpillar

'Look what Mr Gill has given us,' said Miss Mee one day. She held out a small round flat tin with a glass lid.

'Can't see nowt,' said Paul.

'No,' agreed Imdad, shaking his head.

'There's some little yellow ball things,' said Wendy, peering into the tin with her eyes screwed up.

'I'll let you see them properly later,' said Miss Mee. 'We'll get out the magnifying glass and look at them close up. Mr Gill found them on his cabbages.'

'What are they?' asked Asif.

'Eggs,' said Miss Mee. 'I think a butterfly laid them on Mr Gill's cabbages, then flew away and left them there. I expect they'll hatch soon. We'll keep an eye on them over the next few days and see what happens.'

She put the tiny yellow eggs on a large

cabbage leaf and left them on a table at the side of the classroom. Everyone had a turn at looking at them through the magnifying glass. 'They're like yellow hand grenades,' said Asif. They were too.

A few days later Jean was walking past the table, when she suddenly gave a loud squeak. 'Miss Mee! Miss Me-ee! There's little caterpillars on the cabbage.' Everyone rushed over to see: two of the little eggs had hatched, and there were two tiny green caterpillars crawling across the cabbage leaf.

Next day the tiny caterpillars seemed to be just a little bigger and stronger. The cabbage leaf had big, ragged holes all over it. 'They've been busy eating all night while you were asleep,' explained Miss Mee. 'They'll soon need fresh cabbage leaves, or they might crawl away to look for some.'

'They don't know the way to the garden,' said Gary.

'No, but they might just crawl all

round our classroom, looking for cabbages,' said Miss Mee. 'And they might get lost on the way.'

One caterpillar was bigger than the other. The children decided to call the little one Jack and the big one The Giant. Paul brought a fresh cabbage leaf from the allotments the next day, and Mary brought another the next day. Jack and The Giant grew bigger and stronger. Now the children could see a yellow stripe down their green backs. The caterpillars could travel very fast, crawling and then making a loop with their backs, so that their back legs caught up with all their front legs. Then off they went, crawling and looping again.

The next morning when everyone came in, the cabbage leaves were dry and full of holes, like old rags. Jack and The Giant were nowhere to be seen.

'They've gone,' said everyone. 'Where's Jack and The Giant? They've gone!'

'Watch where you walk,' said Miss Mee. 'They might have crawled down on to the floor, and it would be dreadful if we trod on them by accident. Or they might be hiding on the ceiling somewhere.' The children looked everywhere; it was like a game of Hunt the Thimble, but this was Hunt the Caterpillar instead. They looked under the sand tray, in the Play House, in the brick box, behind Miss Mee's table, near the record player, among the library books, even in the dolls' house. But Jack and The Giant were nowhere to be seen.

The children were really sad. They thought perhaps a bird might have hopped in at the window and gobbled up their caterpillars. And none of the other little yellow eggs had hatched out at all. Then, gradually, the children forgot about their two little green pets. Autumn came, and winter, and snow. Lots of people caught measles and had to stay away from school.

Then, slowly, it grew warmer again.
The bulbs in bowls in the window-sill
shot up into beautiful golden daffodils.

One day the clock stopped. 'It must
need new batteries,' said Miss Mee. She
lifted it down from its hook. 'Oh!' she
said. Everyone looked up. 'Guess who's
been hiding at the back of the clock,' said
Miss Mee. It was Jack and The Giant.
She turned the clock round so that
everyone could see.

'They're not caterpillars,' said Asif.

37

'They're kind of brown bundles,' said Laura.

'Where's Jack and The Giant?' asked Larry in a disappointed voice.

'They're inside those brown bundles,' said Miss Mee. 'They're not caterpillars any more—they're pupae. They crawled up the wall and hid behind the clock, then they made those kind of brown blankets to wrap themselves in during the winter, like sleeping-bags. Now it's springtime and they'll want to get out. They won't want to be pupae any more.' Miss Mee left the clock upside down on the table so that everyone could see how Jack and The Giant had wrapped themselves up in snug brown bundles.

One sunny morning soon afterwards Paul saw one pupa move. Later on, the other pupa looked as though it was wriggling inside. 'They want to get out and fly in the sunshine,' said Miss Mee.

'Caterpillars can't fly,' said Wendy.

They watched the little brown bundles

still stuck to the back of the clock. Something was trying to creep out of one. Slowly, very sl-o-w-ly, some sort of insect was pulling itself out of the brown sleeping-bag. It walked to the end of the clock and sat there trembling for a while.

Then it little by little shook open its wings and held them outstretched. They were white, with smudges of black and black tips.

'It's a butterfly!' said everyone.

'Jack's a butterfly! He's changed into a butterfly.' They watched him take off and flutter out of the open window. That afternoon The Giant struggled out of his pupa case too and sat with outstretched wings on the clock. Then he too fluttered out into the sunny playground. Perhaps he was going to look for Jack.

5
A Hallowe'en Happening

Everyone in Miss Mee's class was very busy. It was Hallowe'en, and they were decorating the classroom with scary things.

Jean and the twins Barbara and Rosemary were cutting out black cats and then sticking bright green paper behind to shine through the eyeholes. The cats were going to go up on the windows.

Ian and Michael were cutting out big fat spooky shapes and making large eyeholes: they were going to be masks. Ian tried one over his face and scared Mr Loftus, who was just passing the window with a ladder.

Paul and Pete had already painted some white skeletons on black paper and

now Miss Mee was hanging them from the ceiling, where they swayed and danced.

Wendy, Nasreen and Asif had painted egg-boxes black, and now they were twisting on hairy black pipe-cleaners for legs—these were going to be giant, man-eating spiders to hang from the classroom ceiling *just* inside the door. 'When one of these brushes against someone, I bet they nearly jump out of their skin!' said Asif.

Brenda, Imdad and Sue were making black crêpe paper clothes for some dolly pegs. They were going to be witches with pointed black hats and wild hair made out of bristles from the classroom brush.

Little Larry was talking to himself as he drew things to go into a spell: 'A eyelash and a egg and a owl's feather...'

Outside the windows of the class-room, the sky seemed to be growing darker as great grey clouds rolled overhead. The wind was whistling round the corner of the school and coming in through the cracks between the windows. It made the skeletons shiver and tremble on their strings.

Miss Mee climbed down off the table and put some music in the tape recorder. It was music they liked to listen to in the hall: first the clock striking twelve, then the skeletons coming to life and dancing, slow at first, then faster and faster and wilder and wilder until the cock crew and the skeletons melted away into the morning mist.

'It's the skelly music,' said the children, pleased, but they were glad the classroom lights were bright and they were all together.

The music was very faint; the clock had just finished striking and the first skellies were stretching and walking on tip-toe before they started to dance.

'A toe-bone and a finger-bone,' said little Larry, still drawing his spell. The children listened to the music growing faster.

Suddenly, they all stopped work and looked round with big eyes. There was a strange noise: a loud thumping, like giant footsteps, then a lo-o-o-ong scraping noise and a short scream. Everyone—Miss Mee too—heard the dreadful sounds and held their breath. The loud creaking giant footsteps began again, then gradually died away.

The wind whistled even more loudly outside; now the skellies were dancing madly in the music, and the painted skellies were swaying and turning with them, grinning their great white painted grins. Everyone was sitting very quiet, forgetting their work. 'A flitty bat and a creepy spider,' murmured little Larry.

Click! The lights went out, suddenly. Everyone gasped. The classroom was quite dark. No one moved. Miss Mee quickly reached into her drawer for the birthday candle and the matches. She stood the candle in its holder on her desk. Its white flame quivered. 'Aaaahh...' said everyone, watching it and feeling better.

The cock crew very faintly and the

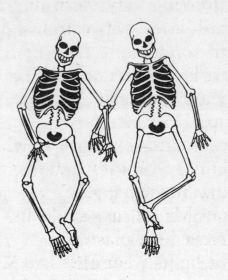

skellies began to tip-toe away with the music and disappear.

Click! Without any warning the lights came back on. Everyone started to chatter and smile again. 'Buttercups and daisies and silver stars,' said Larry still drawing.

Mr Loftus opened the classroom door and a black spider brushed against him. Everyone laughed loudly, but Mr Loftus didn't laugh at all. He came over to Miss Mee looking very stern and holding a football boot between his finger and thumb.

'Just look what some joker threw up on the roof,' he said. 'I expect you heard me up there just now. The boot was jammed in the television aerial. I gave it a good tug and cut my hand on the wire— my, that made me yell!'

'Poor Mr Loftus,' said Miss Mee, and she fetched the plasters.

'The lights went off,' said Wendy.

'Yes, that was while I was mending the aerial,' explained Mr Loftus. 'I had to switch off at the mains for a minute.'

He looked round at everyone. 'You weren't worried, were you?'

'No, oh no, course not...!' cried

everyone quickly. But the painted skellies swayed and nudged each other, grinning their wide, white grins. *They* knew.

6
'Whose Is It?'

It was a sunny afternoon in summer.
Soon it would be Sports Day, and Miss
Mee's class were out on the field practis-
ing for the races. Miss Mee had her
whistle round her neck on a string and
she was showing her class what they
would have to do on Sports Day.

'Do you see these long, straight lines
Mr Loftus has made on the grass?' she
asked.

'I saw him,' said Pete. 'He was pulling
a paint machine, like men have for
making lines down the middle of the
road.'

'Well, Mr Loftus has made sort of
roads for you to run down,' said Miss
Mee. 'They're called lanes...'

'Like Allotment Lane!' shouted
everyone.

'That's right,' said Miss Mee, 'and when it's time to race, you have to run down the lane in front of you as fast as you can, until you get to the finishing line.'

'I can't see the line,' said Imdad.

'It's at the other end,' said Miss Mee. 'But on Sports Day two of the Big Boys will hold a rope across the end of the lanes, and the first person to touch it will win the race.'

'Can we try? Can we race now?' asked everyone.

'We'll let the girls race first,' said Miss Mee. 'Come on, all the girls—there's a running lane for each of you.' The girls began to line up. '*No*, silly girls!' said Miss Mee to Rosemary and Barbara. 'I know you're twins, but you still have to have a lane each to run in.'

At last all the girls were standing in a line, with one foot just behind the white starting line, and the other foot ready to push off.

'Ready—steady—' PEEP! went Miss Mee's whistle. The girls all ran and ran. The boys began to cheer. Laura and Wendy ran in a crooked line and bumped each other and fell down on to the grass in a heap. The boys laughed and cheered again. Jean got to the finishing line first. She was tall and had long legs. The boys cheered again as the girls came skipping back to Miss Mee.

'Phew! I'm sweating,' said Laura. 'Feel my forehead, Miss Mee.'

'You should have taken your woolly off before you started racing. Go and leave them under the trees. Nasreen will look after them.' Nasreen didn't want to race, so she was sitting under the shade of the tall chestnut trees at the edge of the grass.

All the girls undid their cardigans and ran to give them to Nasreen. Then it was the boys' turn to practise running, so they took off their grey pullovers and threw them over to Nasreen to look after.

The boys stood ready to run down their lanes to the finishing line. Ian gave Miss Mee his glasses to look after. 'Keep your toes back off the line,' called Miss Mee to all the boys. Then: 'Ready— Steady—' PEEP! went her whistle.

The boys ran and ran. The girls cheered. The boys' legs and arms were moving like pistons on an express train, as they shot down their lanes to the finishing line.

'Ian's won. Hurray!' shouted the girls, jumping up and down at the side. Miss Mee gave him his glasses back and he blinked at everyone and looked pleased.

Suddenly, they heard the bell ringing in school. 'Merciful heaven,' said Miss Mee. 'That's the bell for home time. Quickly. Get your pullovers and cardigans from Nasreen—we must dash back into school and get your things ready for going home!'

The next morning lots of people in Miss Mee's class came in looking worried. They all came to tell her the same thing.

'I went home with the wrong pullover on.'

'My Mum says this woolly isn't mine.'

'This pullover isn't mine: it touches my knees.'

'Where's my grey cardigan? This one's too tight.'

'My Mum says my pullover's newer than this one I took home.'

Miss Mee asked all the children with other people's woollies on, to stand at the front. There were twelve all together! And they all had a grey pullover or a grey cardigan on. Grey was the colour of the uniform Mr Gill liked everyone to wear.

Miss Mee looked at the twelve at the front. Then she looked at the back collar of all their woollies. 'No name on it!' she said. 'No name. No name on this one either, nor this one. Nor this one. No name on this, or this, or this. Nor this.'

Not one of the twelve grey woollies had a name on. 'It's not surprising that there's been a mix-up,' said Miss Mee sternly. 'When you ran to get your woollies back from Nasreen last night, you didn't have your name in them, so you just grabbed any old woolly. No wonder you've all got someone else's. Tell your Mums: you must have your name on your woolly!'

She told all the twelve to take off the one they were wearing and sit down. One by one, Miss Mee held up the woollies. 'Here's one with a V-neck and a little hole in the elbow.' Michael said it was his. 'Here's a cardigan with a button missing at the bottom.' Barbara said it was hers. 'Here's a pullover with buttons on the shoulder.' Ian said it was his. 'Here's another pullover with a V-neck and a blue label at the back.' Asif said it was his.

In the end they managed to find the right owner for each woolly—but it took a long time and they missed P.E. in the hall.

Miss Mee said, 'There's a little rhyme you'd better all learn; it's a help-you-to-remember rhyme:

What a shame we have some sillies
Who have no name inside their
woollies!'

The next day *everyone* came to school

and showed Miss Mee their names written on the label of their woolly. Every single person! I wonder whether you know any Help-you-to-remember rhymes?

7
Class Party

One morning Wendy came into the class-room carrying a large paper bag with something inside. She looked very excited and pleased with herself as she gave it to Miss Mee. 'It's imbitations.'

'Imbitations?' asked Miss Mee.

'Yes,' nodded Wendy, 'for my party on Sunday.'

'Oh, they're invitations for your party,' said Miss Mee, 'You'll soon be six, won't you? Would you like to give your invitations out, Wendy?'

Wendy went round the room and gave out five invitations to boys and five invitations to girls. The five lucky boys and five lucky girls tore open the envelopes and looked at the cards inside. These were decorated with pictures of sweets and balloons, and a clown was waving to them to come to Wendy's party. Miss Mee read Sue's invitation out loud.

'Dear Sue,
Please will you come to my party on Sunday.
It will be from 3 o'clock to 6 o'clock at 7, Park Road.
Love from Wendy.'

'Oooh!' said the ten lucky ones excitedly, and they began to chatter to Wendy.

'It's going to be a *great* big party,' she said. 'A magician's going to come and do magic and tricks, and we're going to have a *great* big cake in the shape of a teddy bear, and there's going to be party hats and games to play and sweets for everyone.'

'It's *my* birthday on Friday,' said Jean. 'I'll be six too.' Miss Mee looked at the register and found Jean's birthday written in there.

'So you are, Jean, you're going to be

six too. Are you going to have a party like Wendy?'

Jean shook her head. 'Mum says I can't.' She looked very disappointed.

Miss Mee said to everyone, 'We've got two birthdays this week. Jean and Wendy are both going to be six. Wendy's going to have a super party at home, so we'll have Jean's party here: we'll have a class party.'

'Hurray!' said everyone, and Jean cheered up straight away.

'We'd better have invitations like Wendy,' said Miss Mee. She gave everyone a card and they carefully wrote:

'Please come to a party in Class 1 on Friday afternoon.'

Most people copied it from the black-board, except little Larry who wrote over the top of Miss Mee's writing on his card. Then they decorated the cards with anything they liked: some had stars and flowers, some had cats and rabbits, some had rockets and dinosaurs and helicopters and monsters.

Everyone chose a friend to swop invitations with.

'Has anyone not got one?' asked Miss Mee. Everyone had. 'Good,' said Miss Mee, 'then that means you're *all* invited to our party on Friday afternoon.'

The next day Miss Mee brought in some long strips of sugar paper. They were cut in ups and downs all along one edge.

'Like a saw,' said Imdad.

'Like a dragon's back,' said Laura.

'Like wigwams,' said Ian.

'Like Jaws' teeth,' said Paul.

Miss Mee took one of the pieces and wrapped it round her head. 'It's for a crown. For a crown!' shouted everyone.

'Party hats,' said Miss Mee. After that everyone was busy cutting out pieces of silver paper and tissue paper to decorate their crowns. Miss Mee stapled each one into a circle to fit a head, and they were left overnight for the glue on the jewels to dry.

The next day was Friday and everyone was very excited, waiting for the Party Afternoon. Soon after register time Miss Mee put dancing music on the tape recorder and everyone jigged and jogged and flipped and flopped and got very out of breath. Sometimes their crowns fell off but that just made it all more fun.

Then they played musical statues and then the Golden Goose Game, in which you had to try to make someone laugh. Jean and Wendy both had a turn at being the princess, but some of the boys nearly turned their faces inside out trying to look horrible and Jean and Wendy both laughed out loud.

Then they all made a semicircle of chairs. 'It's like a horse-shoe,' said Ian.

'For good luck,' said Pete.

'Yes, for my birthday,' said Wendy.

'*And* Jean's!' said everyone else.

When they were all sitting down Miss

Mee lit a big candle in a candle holder.
'We'll sing to the birthday girls,' she said
and most people joined in:

> *'Happy birthday to you,*
> *Happy birthday to you,*
> *Happy birthday, dear Jean,*
> *Happy birthday to you!'*

Then they sang the same again, but to
Wendy this time. Then some of the boys
began to sing:

> *'Happy birthday to you,*
> *Squashed tomatoes and stew,*
> *Bread and butter in the gutter,*
> *Happy birthday to you!'*

Then they sang another song:

> *'Happy birthday to you,*
> *I went to the zoo,*
> *I saw a fat monkey,*
> *And I thought it was you!'*

Jean thought this was very funny and

laughed and laughed. She blew out the candle and everyone gave loud claps for her and Wendy and a Hip, Hip, HooRAY shout.

Then Miss Mee handed round the plates. They weren't real plates, they were chocolate biscuit plates. 'Better than ordinary plates,' said everyone. 'You can eat these!' On to each plate Miss Mee put a little pile of dolly mixtures. Last of all she fetched a tray and handed everyone a paper cup of orange juice.

Jean was holding her dolly mixtures tightly in her hand. They were going squishy, and her hand was growing sticky, but she didn't mind. When the party was over, she was going to run straight home to share them with her Mum and the baby.

Michael squinted up into his cup as he waited for the last drop of orange to fall on to his tongue.

'This is a good party,' he said.

'Yes, 'tis,' said Jean. 'The best I've ever had.'

'I'm glad,' said Miss Mee.

8
School Photograph

Miss Mee had some news for her class. 'Tomorrow the school photographer is coming,' she said. 'He'll take a picture of each one of you, so don't forget to come to school looking really clean and tidy.'

Michael ran home to tell the news. 'We're having our photo taken at school tomorrow,' he shouted to his mother. 'We've got to look really clean and tidy. Miss Mee said.'

'Of course,' said his mother. 'I'll get your best white shirt ready.'

Michael shouted to his Dad, 'Did you hear that, Dad? We're having our photo taken in school tomorrow.'

'You'd better look your best then,' said his Dad. 'I'll polish your shoes so you can see your face in them.'

'Thanks, Dad,' said Michael.

He ran upstairs to tell his grandmother the news. 'What a good thing
I've just finished this new pullover for
you,' said his grandmother. 'You can
wear it over the top of your white shirt.'

Michael ran out to the back yard. His
Grandad was there, seeing to Squeaker,
the white mouse. Michael told him the
news. 'You'll have to tidy yourself up for
that then,' said Grandad, looking
Michael up and down. 'You don't
usually look very tidy.'

Michael let Squeaker run up his arm
and round his neck. Then he held him on
his hand and just looked at him.
Squeaker squeaked loudly and looked
back at Michael with his bright eyes.

Next morning Michael's mother
helped him on with his white shirt. The
collar was very stiff and the buttons were
very tight. His father brought in his
shoes. 'You can see your face in them,
Michael,' he said. 'Plenty of spit and
polish, that's what you need for a good

shine.' Michael put the shoes on and his Dad did them up tightly for him.

His grandmother came downstairs. 'Look at your lovely new pullover, Michael,' she said. 'Haven't I made it nicely for you? Let's put it on.' And she and his mother pulled the new pullover over Michael's head. It was very tight and Michael felt very hot and uncomfortable. He didn't much like the pattern on the pullover either, it was very bright. He wished it was grey like the other boys' pullovers, but he didn't say anything. He set off for school. They all watched him go.

'Smile nicely for the photographer,' called Grandma, as they waved him off. When he got round the corner, he met his Grandad, waiting for him.

'Thought you might like Squeaker for luck,' said Grandad, and he put the little white mouse into Michael's scrubbed clean hands. Michael put Squeaker in the pocket of his best grey trousers.

68

He had a very busy day at school. First Miss Mee asked him to finish his number work. Then she said he could paint the model boat he'd been making out of old boxes (she didn't know Squeaker was in his pocket all the time). Later on, he played football in the school playground; the new pullover made a lovely bright goalpost. Two stray dogs got into the playground, and Michael helped to sort out the fight. One of the dogs tore a hole in the new pullover with its teeth.

After that Michael let Squeaker have a run on the grass, and they both got rather muddy. Michael had to take him into the washroom and clean him up. But Miss Mee still didn't know that Squeaker was in his pocket. After that the bell rang, and it was time to see the photographer.

When it was Michael's turn to be photographed, he let Squeaker sit on his shoulder. He sat in the chair and smiled at the man. He felt fine.

The next week Miss Mee brought the photos into the classroom. 'They're ready,' she said. 'You can take them home.'

At home everybody looked at Michael's photo.

'Oh, Michael—look at your shirt,' said his mother.

'Oh, Michael—look at your pullover,' said grandmother.

'Look at your socks round your ankles,' said his father.

But his Grandad said, 'That's the best photo of you and Squeaker I've ever seen —I told you he'd bring you luck!'

9
Larry's Snack

'I've got two chews,' said Laura.

'I've got a lollipop,' said Paul.

'I've got three jelly babies,' said Michael.

'I've got one of my Grandad's black bullets,' said Gary.

'I've got a peanut-butter-on-toast sandwich,' said Mary.

'We've got packets of Moondust,' said Rosemary and Barbara.

'I've got an apple,' said little Larry.

'Well, put them all straight in the snack box,' said Miss Mee. 'They're for the afternoon, not the morning. Mrs Eccles likes you to have empty tummies in the morning, so that you eat up all the school dinners she makes.'

She pointed to the snack box on the table near the door. As the children came in every morning, they knew they had to put their snacks in there. It was a fairly large cardboard box. The children had decorated it with pictures of chocolates, biscuits and fruit cut out of a catalogue.

At afternoon playtime Miss Mee took the lid off the box and said, 'Who brought two chews?'

'I did,' said Laura.

'Who brought a lollipop?' asked Miss Mee.

'I did,' said Paul.

'Who brought three jelly babies?'

'I did,' said Michael.

'Who brought a black bullet?'

'I did,' said Gary.

'Who brought a peanut-butter-on-toast sandwich?'

'I did,' said Mary.

'Who brought packets of Moondust?'

'We did,' said Rosemary and Barbara.

'Who brought an apple?'

'Me,' said Larry.

All the snacks were eventually sorted

out and they went out into the playground. 'I don't really want an apple,'
said Larry.

'*I'll* have it,' said Laura. 'You can have
one of my chews.' Larry took one of the
pink chews wrapped in paper and
started to open it.

'Want a jelly baby?' asked Michael.

'A black one?' asked Larry.

'Yeh, all right – if you give me that
chew,' said Michael.

'Great!' said Larry, and he took the
black jelly baby.

Paul came round the corner with his
lollipop. 'Ooh, you got a black jelly
baby?' he asked. 'Give us it – you can
have this lolly.' Larry thought that was a
good bargain: the lolly would last much
longer than the jelly baby, even a black
one. He handed it over to Paul and took
the lollipop. He started to lick it. It was
green: lime. A bit sour, really.

'Want some of our Moondust?' asked
the twins. They were tipping the

74

Moondust out of the silver packets on to their hands and licking it with the tips of their pink tongues.

'It's lovely,' said Barbara. 'It tickles behind your teeth.'

Larry was dying to try some. 'You can have this lolly if you give me the rest of your packet,' he said.

'O.K.' said Barbara. 'I'll have the lolly; Rosemary's still got her packet left.' She gave Larry her half-empty packet.

Larry tipped some of the Moondust on to his hand. It was a green powder and it sparkled. He tried a tiny bit on the tip of his tongue. It *did* tickle behind his teeth, and all over his tongue as well. It was very peculiar.

'What's it like, that Moondust stuff?' asked Gary.

'Tickly,' said Larry.

'That's nothing,' boasted Gary. 'My Grandad's black bullets are so hot they can make you feel warm all over, my Grandad says.'

'Let's have one, then,' said Larry.

'I'll swop it for the rest of that Moondust,' said Gary.

Larry shook the packet. There wasn't much left in it. One of Gary's Grandad's black bullets would be a good swop. They swopped over. Larry looked at the black bullet Gary gave him. 'It's not black!' he said. 'It's kind of brown!'

'Doesn't matter,' said Gary. 'It's just what they're called: *black* bullets.'

'I don't want a brown black bullet,' complained Larry.

'Allavit!' said Mary, who had been listening. Her mouth was full of her first big bite of peanut-butter-on-toast sandwich. In her hand she was holding the rest of the sandwich; now it was shaped like a bridge where she'd bitten out a hole in the middle. Larry liked the look of the bridge shape. And he'd never ever eaten peanut-butter-on-toast sand-wiches before.

'Here y'are then,' he said, putting the

sticky brown black bullet in Mary's hand. She gave him the bridge-shaped sandwich. He carefully took another bite and made the hole under the bridge wider. He chewed for a moment, then said, 'Eeuggh! That's puky!' which wasn't at all nice.

'Peanut butter's lovely,' said Mary.

'Yes, 'tis,' nodded her friend, Laura. '*I* like it.'

'You have it then,' said Larry.

'All right, I will,' said Laura. 'And you can have your apple back. I've only eaten half of it – it's bitter.'

Larry took the half apple. It didn't look at all bitter to him. It was red and yellow and juicy-looking. He took a big bite. Mmmm, yummy. An apple was *just* the thing for a snack!

Imdad's Saturday

'Don't come to school on Saturdays or Sundays,' Miss Mee told her class, 'because you won't get in! Mr Loftus, the caretaker, always bolts the gate and locks all the doors at the weekend. The school is empty—and if Mr Loftus hears noises, he thinks it's burglars! So, remember: Saturdays and Sundays are holidays.'

But Saturday was never a holiday for Imdad: it was the busiest day of the week for him. His Dad and Mum woke him early in the morning, and after a quick breakfast, they all drove in their long red van to the market not far from Allotment Lane School.

Then the hard work really began. First of all Imdad had to help his father to build the stall. They pulled long metal bars through the doors in the back of the van and screwed them tightly together to make a stall shape. Some of the bars stood up tall to make the sides and roof, the other bars went across to make the counter where they were going to put all the things they had to sell.

After they had made the frame of the stall, they had to pull the heavy roof-cloth out of the van. Imdad's mother and father pulled it right over the back and sides and roof of the stall, so that if it rained, they would stay dry, and so would the clothes they sold on their stall.

Last of all, they pulled some planks of wood out of the van and laid them across the metal bars to make a table; that's where they were going to lay out all the clothes ready to sell.

Now the stall was ready; the worst job was done. Imdad's Mum smiled at him. She was very pretty and loved to wear lots of metal bracelets that tinkled when she moved. 'Now we'd better fetch the boxes, Imdad,' she said. Imdad ran to the van and carried back four boxes, one on top of another—he could just peep over the top. His mother took them from him and put them at the side of the stall. Then Imdad arranged them neatly side by side with the labels showing, so that all the people passing by could see the prices.

Imdad fetched more and more and more. There were boxes of vests and pants, boxes of tights and lacy petti-coats, there were all sorts and sizes and colours of knee socks and ankle socks and babies' bootees. There were bibs and nappies. There were cardigans and pull-overs. There were all sorts of T-shirts for boys and girls, some with the Muppets on, some with Winnie the Pooh, some with jungle animals or Superman or racing cars—and hundreds of others.

Imdad's Mum and Dad were hanging

jeans and skirts on hangers, and hooking them over the roof bars.

At the back of the counter was a big tin; that was where they put the money if someone bought something. Imdad often put people's money in the tin—he could even give them the right change if they gave him too much money to start with.

It was a beautiful stall, and most people stopped to look or buy. Imdad thought it was the best stall on the market.

One Saturday the sun was shining and the market was very busy. Mrs Eccles, the cook from Allotment Lane School, came past. She smiled at Imdad. 'Hello, Imdad—are you helping your Mum and Dad? Can you help me as well? I want a little present for a baby I know. What do you think would be nice?' Imdad helped her to choose a white cardigan, and Mrs Eccles went away very pleased. Imdad put the money in the tin.

Then Miss Mee came along. 'Hello, Imdad!' she said. 'I'm just looking for some new tights—can you help me to find some the right size?' Imdad looked in the boxes of tights and found just what Miss Mee wanted. He put the tights into a white paper bag and took the money. 'Thank you, Imdad,' said Miss Mee. 'See you on Monday at school.'

The next customers were Brenda and her mother. They smiled at Imdad and stopped to look at everything. 'Ooh, look at those socks, Mummy!' said Brenda. 'They've got toes in, like fingers in gloves. Aren't they funny?' She held up one of the toe-socks for her mother to see. 'Look, they've got a different colour for each toe: a purple big toe, then a pink one, then a red one, then an orange one, then a black little toe. Oh, I wish *I* had a pair of these socks, they're the prettiest I've ever seen.'

'Yes, they *are* nice, aren't they?' said

Brenda's mother, and she opened her purse to see how much money she had left, when suddenly there was a cla-a-a-nng, and a loud shout.

'Oh! My mother!' cried Imdad, rushing to help her. One of the side bars of the stall had fallen down, right on to her foot. She was holding on to the stall, lifting her bruised foot off the ground and groaning, 'Oh! Oh! My foot—it hurts.' Imdad's father put his arm round her to stop her falling over.

Brenda's mother said, 'You should go to hospital—you may have broken a bone in your foot.'

Imdad's father looked very worried. 'Yes,' he said, 'but I cannot leave the stall.'

'I could manage it, Dad!' said Imdad. 'I know where everything is.'

'Perhaps *we* could help Imdad,' said Brenda to her mother. 'Imdad could tell us what to do.'

Brenda's mother thought for a

moment. 'Mm—yes, I'm sure we could. May we help Imdad?' she asked his father.

'Oh, yes, please—my poor wife's foot is already swelling a great deal. I will quickly take her to the hospital in our van.'

So Imdad was left in charge of the stall with Brenda and her mother to help him. Brenda thought it was lovely—just like her games of playing shops. She helped to take the money and put it in the tin; she arranged all the bibs and pretty little dresses; she put all the socks straight and counted all the toes on the toe-socks, to make sure they all had just five. Imdad showed her how to hang the tape-measure ready round her neck, in case people wanted to measure themselves for jeans or skirts. Then they both sat underneath the stall counter eating the jam doughnuts that Brenda's mother had bought from the cake stall next to Imdad's.

After quite a long time, Imdad's Mum and Dad came back. This time his mother was smiling again. A nurse at the hospital had bandaged her foot and it was very much better. 'Thank you so much!' said Imdad's father to Brenda and her mother. 'We are tremendously grateful—thank you so much for looking after our stall.'

'It was fun!' said Brenda to Imdad. 'Thank you for letting me help.'

Just before bedtime there was a loud knock at Brenda's front door. She was in her dressing-gown and slippers ready for bed, so she opened the door just a crack. There was Imdad. And she could see their long red van out on the road.

'Hello, Imdad,' she said, and opened the door wide.

'Here's a present for your kind mother,' said Imdad, holding out a *huge* bunch of flowers wrapped in shiny paper and tied with a great big blue bow.

'For me? Oh, how beautiful!' said

Brenda's mother. 'What lovely flowers.'

'And a present for Brenda,' said Imdad, 'because she helped me on the stall.' He gave Brenda a little paper packet. 'You can come and help again if you like—my parents would like you to.' He smiled at Brenda and ran back to the van. He climbed in and waved as his father drove off.

Brenda opened the little paper packet very slowly, feeling it to see whether she could guess what was in it. 'It's very soft,' she said, 'with sort of bumpy bits ... what is it?—Oh! It's a pair of those lovely toe-socks,' she said. 'Oooh, aren't they gorgeous! I'm *glad* we went to the market this Saturday, aren't you, Mum?'

11
Wee Willie Winkie Time

It was news time. Pete stood up and showed everyone his new haircut. It was very short.

'It's like skinheads,' said Paul.

'It's like Yul Brynner,' said Michael. 'He was on telly.'

'I saw him!' shouted everyone. 'It was the Kingneye! He was the king and there were lots of children . . .'

'Who saw *The King and I*?' asked Miss Mee. Nearly everyone put their hands up. 'But it was on *very* late last night,' she said. Then she asked about some other programmes on television.

'Who saw *Police Chase*?' she asked. Some of the class had seen it.

'Who saw the boxing?' she asked. Some of the boys had seen it.

'What did you see last night?' Miss Mee asked Wendy.

'The *'Ammer 'Ouse of 'Orror*,' said Wendy. 'There was blood coming out of all the taps. It gave me bad dreams and I woke my Dad, screaming!'

'When did you go to bed, Jean?' asked Miss Mee.

'Same time as me Mum,' said Jean, yawning.

'When did you go to bed, Pete?' asked Miss Mee.

'After the boxing,' said Pete. 'I went to bed when he was knocked out in the fifth round. His eye was all cut an' he just lay there groaning...'

Miss Mee thought everyone was going to bed much too late. She said, 'You must all get plenty of sleep, or you won't grow big and strong. You'll stay thin and small and your faces will be pale...'

'Palefaces!' cried Gary. 'There was a Western on telly the other night, it was the Midnight Movie, and—'

'Midnight!' said Miss Mee. 'That's *far* too late! You should all be in bed by eight o'clock!'

'Like Wee Willie Winkie,' said Ian.

'Yes,' said Miss Mee. 'Can you remember about Wee Willie Winkie?' Some of the children did; they chanted:

'Wee Willie Winkie runs through
    the town,
Upstairs and downstairs in his
    nightgown,
Knocking at the window, calling
    through the lock:
'Are all the children in their beds?
    —It's past eight o'clock!'

At story time that day Miss Mee told her class a story; it was about a princess called Sleeping Beauty. Miss Mee came to the part of the story where the princess pricked her finger and fell fast asleep. '—And the cook and the kitchen boy fell asleep, and the horses in the stable fell asleep. The King and the

91

Queen fell asleep, and the soldiers on the battlements fell asleep. The cats and the dogs fell asleep, and even the birds on the window-sills fell asleep—'

Miss Mee suddenly stopped.

Everyone was sitting listening on the Story Carpet. Pete was sitting in the middle, but his eyes were closed and his head was nodding to one side. The rest of the class turned to look at him. His mouth was open, and in the quiet room they all heard him give a little snore...

'Merciful heavens,' said Miss Mee. 'I think Pete is ready for bed. In fact, I think you're nearly *all* ready for bed. We'll have to do something about your bedtimes!'

The next day Miss Mee's class started work on a huge wall picture. First of all, they had to choose what to make with cardboard and polystyrene boxes. They were going to cover one wall of the classroom with a town.

'We need lots of houses,' said Larry,

'with chimneys and telly aerials and doors and windows.'

'And a school,' said Laura, 'with a playground and conker trees.'

'And lots of shops,' said Ian, 'with things in the windows.'

'Bagsy draw the toyshop!' said Paul quickly.

'Bagsy draw the garage and all the cars,' said Michael.

'We could have a pub,' said Jean, 'for the Dads.'

'And a fish and chip shop,' said Asif.

'And a church,' said Paul, 'with a clock on the tower.'

'And the clock says eight o'clock!' said Mary.

'What a lot of marvellous ideas,' said Miss Mee. 'And I think we'd better paint lots of children getting ready for bed, and last of all, we'll paint a very big Wee Willie—'

'*Winkie*!' shouted everyone.

'And he's running very fast,' said

Wendy. 'And there are lots of stairs for him to go up and down and he keeps looking in all the bedroom windows and shouting: 'Are all the children in their beds?'

'It's past eight o'clock!' finished everyone else.

'Good,' said Miss Mee. 'We'll start straight away. But first of all, I've got two questions for you—what time is Wee Willie Winkie time?'

'Eight o'clock!' said everyone.

'And where does Wee Willie Winkie want you to go at eight o'clock?'

'To bed!' said everyone.

'We'll see who can remember that tonight,' said Miss Mee. 'But now, let's get out the paints and paper and start work.'

12
A Class Trip

It was early on a hot summer's morning. Excited children from Miss Mee's class were already waiting to come into the playground at eight o'clock.

'I'll just unlock the gate,' said Mr Loftus, jangling a bunch of keys. 'I've never known children queue up for school before—what do you want to come to school so early for?'

'It's our trip day!' said Michael. 'We're going to the seaside in a coach.'

'Yes, with three on a seat, we can sit where we like, Miss Mee said,' gasped out Jean, all in one breath. 'And I've got a can of coke and corned beef sarneys and a chocolate biscuit and—'

'That's nothing,' boasted Gary. 'I've got a yoghurt and a spoon and two chocolate biscuits and a bag of lamb 'n mint sauce crisps and—'

Just then they all spotted Miss Mee walking across the playground with a haversack on her back. 'Miss Mee. Miss Mee!' they shouted, and raced across to talk to her.

'What's in *your* bag, Miss Mee?' they asked.

'All sorts,' said Miss Mee.

'Liquorice allsorts?' asked Mary.

'No, just all sorts of things,' said Miss Mee. 'You'll see.'

After that, more and more people arrived and they waited in their class-room for the coach to pull up outside. While they waited, Miss Mee made sure they all had a picnic and money for an ice-cream, and then she made sure they'd all been to the toilet.

'Can we start our picnic now?' asked Nasreen. 'I'm hungry.'

'No,' said Miss Mee. 'Let your break-fast go down first.'

At last the coach arrived and the driver

sounded his horn: Berr-berr! The children cheered: 'Hurray!' They gathered up their bags and went out to the coach.

The headmaster, Mr Gill, was there to see them off. 'Have a lovely time,' he said. 'Drive carefully, Albert. And don't lose anyone, Miss Mee!'

Albert started the bus and the children waved goodbye to Mrs Hubb, the school secretary, in her office, and they knocked on the coach windows at Mr Loftus who was standing at the gate to see them off (and making sure that Albert didn't scratch the school's newly painted gate-posts as he drove the coach through). Then, as the coach rolled down the hill, they all waved at their Mums and Grans and little brothers and sisters who were standing in the doorways to see them set off.

The coach was very, very hot, even though the roof was open and the breeze was blowing people's hair all over their faces. 'Can we start our picnic now?' asked little Larry. 'I'm hungry.'

'No,' said Miss Mee. 'Let your breakfast go down a bit further first.'

'My drink has spilt,' said Nasreen. 'I opened the top to make sure it was all there, and it spilt itself!'

Miss Mee opened her bag and took out a box of paper hankies. She helped to wipe the spilt orange juice off Nasreen's knees and off her shoes.

'My chocolate's melting,' said Ian. 'I was holding the bar in my hand so it wouldn't fall on the floor, and it's melting inside the silver paper!'

Miss Mee opened her bag again and took out an empty plastic bag. 'Put it in here,' she said to Ian. 'Then it won't matter if it melts.' Ian pushed the melting chocolate bar inside the clean plastic bag and put the bag inside his picnic box. He sucked the melted left-overs off his fingers.

'I feel sick,' said Wendy.

'Come and sit with me at the front,' said Miss Mee. 'You can watch Albert driving.'

'I can see the sea!' shouted Paul.

'*I* can see the sea,' shouted Michael. 'I saw it first.'

'No you didn't,' shouted Paul. 'I saw it before you.'

'Stop fighting, you two,' said Miss Mee, 'or I might leave you on the coach with Albert.'

'Yeah! Watch it, you two!' said Albert over his shoulder. Michael and Paul decided to stop shouting at each other. They didn't want to miss going on the beach. The coach stopped in a car park. Miss Mee counted all her children. Then everyone climbed out of the coach, clutching bags and buckets and spades.

'See you here at two o'clock,' called Albert, and drove off.

They ran on to the sand and dumped their things. Then everyone wanted to paddle straight away. 'Put your swimming things on if you've brought them,' said Miss Mee. 'I'll help you if you can't manage yourselves.'

'I've forgotten my swim suit,' moaned Brenda.

'Well, tuck your dress into your pants,' said Miss Mee. That was easily done, and Brenda ran down to splash in the waves with the others.

'Ouch!' shouted Stevie. 'A crab pinched my toes.'

An extra big wave came up behind Imdad and knocked him on to his tummy in the water. 'I'm surfing,' he shouted. 'Look, I'm surfing!'

Wendy trod on a bumpy pebble and sat down suddenly in the water. 'Oh, Miss Mee, my pants are soaked,' she howled. Miss Mee fished in her haversack.

'What a good thing I brought all sorts,' she said. 'Even spare pants!' She helped Wendy change her pants and laid out the wet ones to dry in the sun.

Sue ran along the beach screaming 'Help! Help!' A little seaside donkey was trying to be friendly, following her to have its nose stroked. Sue wasn't used to donkeys. The donkey man came running up and caught the donkey by its reins. He showed Sue how to pat it and hold out a sugar lump on her flat hand.

'There you are,' said the donkey man. 'Prince only wanted to be friendly, you see.' Sue cheered up then, and all the other children thought she was very lucky.

'Can we eat our picnic now?' asked Larry. 'My breakfast's gone right down now.'

'In half an hour,' said Miss Mee.

Ian and Imdad started to make a sand-castle. It was a huge one, with pot-pie towers at each corner. Paul came and showed them how to make a moat all around the castle. Then the three boys raced to and fro to the waves, carrying bucketfuls of water to fill the moat. Then they dug a tunnel underneath the castle, scooping out the sand with their hands. It took ages to make, and just as they sat back on their heels to admire it, two large dogs came pelting across the beach and straight over the top of the castle. It was quite squashed. 'I'm tired of castles,' said Ian. 'Let's dig a hole instead.'

Mary went to the ice-cream van and bought a lolly. It was like a rocket, in stripes of red, yellow and orange. Mary ate half of it, but then it began to melt in the hot sunshine, and it fell off the stick into the sand. 'Eughh!' said Mary. 'I don't want a sandy lolly.' So she buried the melting bits in a hole in the sand.

Asif bought a toffee apple. It was crunchy outside and soft inside, and very very sticky. Asif got toffee round his mouth and on his nose and on his hair. After a while, he put the rest of the toffee apple on his lunch bag. 'I'll just have a wash in the sea,' he said. He ran off and knelt down in the water to splash his sticky face and hair. He ran back, dripping with water—just in time to see a seagull swooping low to snatch the rest of the toffee apple in his beak and fly off with it.

Barbara came limping up to Miss Mee. 'I've cut my toe,' she said. 'There was a sharp shell and I trod on it.'

Miss Mee looked in her bag and found a tube of cream. 'There,' she said, 'that'll make it more comfortable,' and she gently rubbed it in.

'Picnic time!' she called next.

Everyone cheered and raced up to where they had dumped all their belongings. They sat down and opened all the bags and packets and boxes that their Mums had packed for them. Miss Mee had to open lots of cans of lemonade. Some of them had been shaken up in the coach and were too fizzy. They opened with a loud POP! and then swooshed over the top and on to Miss Mee's hands and dripped on to the sand. Miss Mee opened her bag and brought out a damp flannel to wipe herself with. 'What a good thing I brought all sorts,' she said.

Rosemary dropped one of her sandwiches on to the sand. 'Eughh, my egg sandwich is all covered in sand,' she said.

'You've got a sand sandwich,' said Michael. 'Ha, ha, ha!' and he laughed and laughed, and so did Paul and Gary and Pete.

'A sand sandwich,' they laughed.

Rosemary was looking very upset, so her twin, Barbara, said, 'Here's a custard cream—have that instead.' Rosemary cheered up then and ate the custard cream biscuit and took no notice of the boys.

Everyone was just finishing their picnic, when a little breeze started to blow. Dark clouds began to roll across the blue sky and the sun was hidden. It suddenly felt very cold and the breeze blew more and more strongly. Picnic bags began to rustle and dance away along the beach. Mouthfuls of food had gritty sand blown into them, packets of crisps rolled away. Drops of rain, huge and round as pennies, began to fall: splat! on to their picnic boxes, splat! on to the children's bare legs, splat! on to the dry, white sand.

'It's raining,' shouted everyone. 'There's going to be a storm.'

'Oh, it's going to thunder,' cried Wendy, and bust into tears.

'Rubbish!' said Miss Mee. 'Of course it won't thunder. It never does on

Fridays.—Now pack your bags quickly
and pick up your bits and pieces. We'll
go back to the car park and wait for the
coach.'

She watched carefully while everyone
packed their picnic papers and soggy
towels, collections of seagull feathers
and shells, wet bathing costumes,
buckets and spades. They didn't leave a
thing behind (except Mary's melted lolly
and Rosemary's sand sandwich, and
they were buried out of sight anyway).

By now the wind was blowing

everyone along the beach, splattering them with rain. Sand was stinging their legs and arms. They all reached the car park gasping for breath and covered in rain and sand. The car park was quite empty. 'Where shall we go?' asked the children, shivering and jigging up and down.

Berr-berr! came a sudden noise. They all turned their heads—and there was the coach. It slowly roared into the car park, its headlights gleaming through the sheets of rain.

'Hurray!' shouted everyone. Albert stopped the coach and all the children piled in. Miss Mee counted them to make sure no one was missing. Then off drove Albert, back towards school.

'I can still see the sea,' said Paul, looking out of the back window.

'No, you can't,' said Michael.

'Quiet at the back there,' growled Albert, and suddenly the coach was very quiet.

Then Albert switched on the coach radio. It was a pop music programme and most of the children began to sing the hits with the radio.

Miss Mee felt in her large bag and brought out a packet of black and white striped humbugs. 'I forgot I had these,' she said, and offered one to Albert and then to everyone else. The humbugs tasted of peppermint and were so big that they made people's cheeks bulge.

'I-ca-see-der-school,' shouted Michael through his mouthful.

'No-you-cart,' shouted Paul.

'Yes-I-ca.'

'I-ca.'

'I-ca.'

'An-I-ca.'

shouted everyone else, standing up to see.

Albert slowly stopped the coach in front of the school door. It was still pouring with rain. The children had to jump over huge puddles before darting inside, their sandy hair dripping like water-rats' tails.

'Ah, *there* you are again!' said Mr Gill. 'Well, you poor, wet, miserable, frozen creatures—what sort of a day have you had?'

'Oh, great!'

'It was a terrific day.'

'The best trip we've ever had!'

'And how are you, Miss Mee? What sort of a day have *you* had?'

'Great,' said Miss Mee. 'And we've saved you a humbug.'

BRIDGET AND WILLIAM
Jane Gardam

Two horses, two children and two stories of hill farm life. Bridget had William, a shaggy Shetland pony, as round as a partridge, and she was determined to keep him. Susan had Horse, an utterly huge white horse, two hundred years old, cut out of the hillside – and she was determined to save him.

OLGA TAKES CHARGE
Michael Bond

Disaster has struck and Olga da Polga happens to be the only one around who can take charge and save the world – or so she thinks.

TOTTIE: THE STORY OF A DOLLS' HOUSE
Rumer Godden

The Plantaganets don't believe they'll ever move out of their draughty shoe-box, but their owners are given an antique dolls' house like the one Tottie remembers. The dolls are delighted with their new home until haughty Marchpane, a selfish china doll, moves in with them and acts as though she owns the place.

THE DEAD LETTER BOX
Jan Mark

Louie got the idea from an old film which showed how spies left their letters in a secret place – a dead letter box. It was just the kind of thing that she and Glenda needed to help them keep in touch. And she knew the perfect place for it!

DRAGONRISE
Kathryn Cave

What do dragons like to eat best? GIRLS! And when the dragon under Tom's bed told him this, Tom became worried that the poor thing must be starving. Then Tom's elder sister, Sarah, did something that Tom could not forgive – and he realized that the dragon could help him to take a very unusual revenge!

RAGDOLLY ANNA
Jean Kenward

Although she's only made from a morsel of this and a tatter of that, Ragdolly Anna is a very special doll. And within hours of beginning to live with the Little Dressmaker, the White Cat and Dummy, she embarks on some hair-raising adventures. Six delightful stories for children of 5 to 7.

Hello, I'm Smudge

Would you like to hear about my book club?

It's for 4-8 year-olds and you get your own badge, membership book and a Club magazine four times a year.

It's packed with stories, puzzles and competitions.

You get a chance to buy new books!

And there's lots more! For further details and an application form send a stamped, addressed envelope to:

The Junior Puffin Club,
P. O. Box 21,
Cranleigh,
Surrey,
GU6 8UZ